FEARLESSLY PHILIPPE

FEARLESSLY PHILIPPE

By Kiki Thorpe

Illustrated by Laura Catrinella

Disney · HYPERION

Los Angeles   New York

All rights reserved. Published by Disney • Hyperion, an imprint of Buena Vista
Books, Inc. No part of this book may be reproduced or transmitted in any form or by
any means, electronic or mechanical, including photocopying, recording, or by any
information storage and retrieval system, without written permission from the publisher.
For information address Disney • Hyperion, 77 West 66th Street, New York, New York
10023.

First Edition, September 2022
10 9 8 7 6 5 4 3 2 1
FAC-004510-22210
Printed in the United States of America

This book is set in Goudy Old Style Std/Monotype; Laughing Gull/Fontspring
Designed by Samantha Krause
Illustrated by Laura Catrinella
Illustrations created digitally in Adobe Photoshop

Library of Congress Cataloging-in-Publication Data

Names: Thorpe, Kiki, author. • Catrinella, Laura, illustrator.
Title: Fearlessly Philippe / by Kiki Thorpe ; illustrated by Laura
   Catrinella.
Other titles: Beauty and the beast (Motion picture : 1991)
Description: First edition. • Los Angeles ; New York : Disney-Hyperion,
   2022. • Series: Horsetail Hollow ; book 3 • Audience: Ages 5–8. •
   Audience: Grades 2–3. • Summary: Maddie follows her little sister Evie
   into Belle's fairy tale, where Philippe the horse helps them secure
   Belle's happily ever after.
Identifiers: LCCN 2022009898 • ISBN 9781368072267 (hardcover) •
   ISBN 9781368072298 (paperback) • ISBN 9781368073967 (ebook)
Subjects: CYAC: Characters in literature—Fiction. • Horses—Fiction. •
   Wishes—Fiction. • Sisters—Fiction. • Fairy tales—Fiction. •
   LCGFT: Fiction.
Classification: LCC PZ7.T3974 Fe 2022 • DDC [Fic]—dc23
LC record available at https://lccn.loc.gov/2022009898

Reinforced binding for hardcover edition
Visit www.DisneyBooks.com

For Calvin

Maddie Phillips sighed happily. It was a perfect day. The sun was shining. A light breeze blew. And Maddie was in her all-time favorite place—on the back of a horse.

"Giddy-up, Genie." Maddie squeezed her heels to the horse's sides. The dapple gray mare broke into a trot. They jogged once around the ring. Then Genie broke into a smooth canter.

Maddie's mom and little sister, Evie, stood by

the fence, watching. When Maddie rode past, Mom gave her a thumbs-up.

Maddie grinned. Mom hadn't always shared Maddie's love for horses. But little by little, Maddie thought, she was coming around.

Maddie and Genie circled the ring a few more times, then slowed. Maddie walked the horse to where her mom was standing.

Genie's owner, Rosalyn, came over. Her long gray braid swung behind her as she walked. Rosalyn was the Phillipses' closest neighbor. Maddie helped her take care of her horses. In return, Rosalyn sometimes let her ride.

"Genie likes you, I can tell," Rosalyn said as she helped Maddie dismount.

"Really?" Maddie felt a ping of happiness. She couldn't think of a nicer compliment than being liked by a horse.

"She's relaxed with you," Rosalyn said, nodding. "You have a good seat and quiet hands."

3

"Well, I had the best teachers," Maddie said.

"Maddie went to riding camp," Mom explained to Rosalyn.

Maddie just smiled. She wasn't thinking about camp. Her favorite teachers had been two magical horses—Maximus and Angus.

That summer, Maddie's family had moved to a farm called Horsetail Hollow. One day while Maddie and Evie were exploring, they discovered an old well. The well wasn't just any well—it was a wishing well!

The sisters each made a wish—on the same penny. Evie had wished to meet a fairy-tale princess. Maddie had wished for a horse. When a proud white stallion named Maximus showed up, they realized the wishing well had mixed up their wishes. It had brought them a fairy tale horse!

Maximus was the Captain of the Royal Guard in Rapunzel's kingdom. He had galloped right out of Evie's book of fairy tales and into the Phillipses' backyard. But Maddie and Evie soon discovered that without him Rapunzel's story didn't have a happy ending. They had to return Maximus to his fairy tale to make things right again.

The next horse to arrive in Horsetail Hollow was Angus, a handsome black Clydesdale who belonged to Princess Merida. Maddie and Evie had adored Angus, but they knew Merida needed him more. Maddie had been especially sorry to see him go back to his story.

After that, Maddie and Evie had agreed to leave horses in their fairy tales. But Maddie hadn't forgotten their adventures. She thought about them every day.

"Can you all stay for a bit?" Rosalyn asked now. "My son and his family are coming to visit. They should be here any minute. I'd love for you to meet my granddaughter, Macy."

"I wish we could," Mom said. "But we've got to get home. We have a big day tomorrow. It's Evie's birthday."

"I'm going to be seven!" Evie told Rosalyn. "I'm having a tea party!"

"That sounds lovely," Rosalyn said.

"Let me take Genie back to the barn," Maddie told her mom. "Then I'll be ready to go."

In the barn, Maddie took off Genie's bridle. She rinsed the bit and hung it on a hook, then slipped the halter over Genie's head. Genie nibbled Maddie's ponytail in a friendly way.

Maddie patted her and laughed. "Hungry, are you?"

Maddie took off Genie's saddle and blanket. She was putting them away in the tack room, when she heard a voice.

Maddie peeked back into the barn. A girl was standing at Genie's stall. She wore jeans with riding boots. Her hair was braided into many small braids. The girl's eyes were closed. Her forehead lightly rested against Genie's nose.

"Hi," Maddie said.

"Oh!" The girl jumped, startled. "I didn't know anyone was in here."

"I'm Maddie," said Maddie.

The girl nodded. "I know. Gram told me about you. I'm Macy. I was just saying hi to Genie." From the way Genie nuzzled Macy, Maddie could tell they were old friends.

"I know what you want," Macy said to the horse. She took a striped peppermint candy out of her pocket, unwrapped it, and held it out.

"She likes peppermints?" Maddie asked as the horse ate it up. Genie nudged Macy, looking for more.

"She loves them. I always bring some when I visit." Macy wagged her finger at Genie. "Don't be a pig. That's enough for now."

Genie snorted, as if to say, *It was worth a try.*

Maddie held up a currycomb. "I was just going to brush her," she said.

"I can do it," Macy said.

Maddie hesitated. She loved brushing horses. But

she could tell by the eager look on Macy's face that she loved it, too.

Maddie handed the comb to Macy. She watched as Macy brushed Genie's coat with skilled strokes.

"You know," Macy said after a moment, "you look sort of familiar. Did you ever go to Sunny Stables?"

"Riding camp?" Maddie asked. "Yeah! I learned to ride there."

Macy's face lit up. "Me too! We must have been there at the same time."

"Wow, that's so crazy. Remember Coach Hannafin?" Maddie asked.

"How could I forget? 'Fix your hands, young lady!'" Macy said, mimicking their coach's stern voice. "'Are you riding a horse or conducting an orchestra?'"

As the girls were laughing, Rosalyn came into the barn. "Oh good. You two met!" she said when she saw them. "I had a feeling you would like each other."

"Yes. And guess what, Grams," Macy said. "Maddie and I went to the same riding camp!"

"Isn't that something?" Rosalyn put her arm around Macy. Her dark eyes sparkled in their special way. "I knew you girls would have a lot in common. Why don't you come over again tomorrow, Maddie? You and Macy could go riding together."

Maddie suddenly wanted to come more than anything. Since moving to Horsetail Hollow, she hadn't met any kids her own age. And Macy seemed really nice.

But—

"I can't," she said. "It's Evie's birthday."

"Oh, that's right," said Rosalyn. "How could I forget? Evie told me all about it."

Maddie rolled her eyes. "Evie's told *everyone* about it. It's all she can talk about. Hey! Maybe Macy could come? I mean, if you want to . . ."

She trailed off. Why did she think Macy would want to come to a little kid's birthday party?

But to her relief, Macy turned to her grandmother. "Can I, Gram?"

"Of course," Rosalyn said. "Your parents won't mind, Maddie?"

Maddie shook her head. "Evie's friend, Cleo, is driving up from the city. My parents said I could invite a friend, but . . ." She shrugged. "I don't really know anyone around here. It's at eleven o'clock tomorrow."

"I'll be there," Macy said.

"Great!" Maddie waved good-bye and headed outside.

Mom was waiting by the door. "I invited Macy to Evie's party," Maddie told her.

"What a good idea. Speaking of Evie," Mom said, looking around. "Where did she go?"

Maddie spotted her little sister by the paddock. Evie was leaning on the fence, talking to Rosalyn's other horse, Stretch.

"It's going to be a tea party. With *real tea*," Evie was saying as Maddie walked up. "And fancy napkins! And a chocolate cake—with *sprinkles*!"

Stretch nickered. He sounded impressed.

Evie leaned in close, as if to tell him a secret. "And guess what else?"

Stretch's ears turned forward. *What?*

"Belle is coming!" Evie whispered loudly.

"Wait, I thought Cleo was coming. Who's Belle?" Maddie asked.

Evie looked at Maddie. "You know, *Belle*—MY FAVORITE PRINCESS!"

"Princess?" Maddie frowned. "Hold on. Uh-uh. *No way!*"

"What?" Evie asked.

"You can't invite Belle to your party!" Maddie whispered. "Remember all the trouble we caused when we wished for Maximus and Angus? We can't wish anyone out of a fairy tale—*especially* not a princess."

"*I* didn't invite her," Evie said. "Mom did."

"What?!" Maddie exclaimed.

"It's supposed to be a secret," Evie said. "But I heard Mom and Dad talking. Princess Belle is coming to my party! But don't tell Mom that I know. I'm going to act really surprised." Evie clasped her hands together. "Ooh, I just can't wait!"

"Come on, girls. It's time to go!" Mom called.

Evie hopped off the fence and ran to her. Maddie slowly followed, feeling confused. She and Evie had tried to tell Mom and Dad about the wishing well. But their parents hadn't believed them.

Had they changed their minds? Maddie wondered. Were Mom and Dad secretly visiting fairy tales, too?

On the walk back to Horsetail Hollow, Maddie saw her chance to find out. When Evie ran ahead, Maddie turned to Mom.

"Did you invite a *princess* to Evie's party?" she asked.

Mom nodded. "Evie said all she wants for her birthday is tea with a princess. But don't tell Evie about it—it's a surprise!"

Maddie tried to think of another way to ask her question. "But how did you, um . . . meet this princess?"

"I just did an online search," Mom said.

"Princesses are *online?*" Maddie asked.

Mom laughed. "She's not a real princess, Maddie. She's a performer. We hired her to come to Evie's party."

"Oh." Maddie felt silly for thinking a real princess was coming to Evie's party. Still, she was surprised at how disappointed she felt.

"Come on, slowpokes!" Evie yelled. "Last one home is a rotten rutabaga!"

Maddie felt a twinge of worry. Evie might be little, but she was smart. Maddie was pretty sure she could tell a real princess from a fake one.

She just hoped Evie wasn't going to be disappointed, too.

CHAPTER TWO

On Saturday morning, everything was ready for Evie's party. The kitchen table was set for tea. There was a plate of tiny sandwiches and another plate of scones with butter and jam. There was a pot of tea, a little pitcher of milk, and sugar in a silver bowl. A big chocolate cake sat in the middle of the table. HAPPY BIRTHDAY, EVIE! was written on it in pink frosting.

Evie stood by the front window. She pressed her nose to the glass, staring out at the empty road.

"When will they be here?" Evie asked.

"Soon," said Mom. She and Maddie were arranging more little sandwiches on a plate.

"That's what you said the last time I asked!" Evie exclaimed.

Maddie raised an eyebrow. "You mean, two minutes ago?"

Mom smiled. "Try to be patient, Evie. It's a long drive from the city."

"I'm *being* patient. I just wish they would hurry up!" Evie turned from the window and smoothed her dress. She was wearing her favorite princess costume—a puffy yellow ball gown and elbow-length gloves. "Do you think she'll like my dress?" she asked nervously.

"Who, Cleo? Of course she will, honey," Mom said.

Maddie knew Evie didn't mean Cleo. She leaned close and whispered, "You look great. Belle will love it."

Evie beamed.

Outside, a car turned off the main road. It started up the lane to the farm.

"THEY'RE HERE!" Evie yelled.

She raced to the front door and threw it open. Maddie, Mom, and Dad followed her outside.

As soon as the car rolled to a stop, the back door flew open. A small girl with black pigtails hopped out. She was dressed like a princess in an emerald-green gown and matching slippers.

"Evie!" she squealed.

"Cleo!" squealed Evie.

The two friends flew into each other's arms.

"Welcome to Horsetail Hollow," Dad said as Cleo's parents, Mr. and Mrs. Kim, got out of the car. "It's great to see you."

"How was the drive?" Mom asked, giving Cleo's mom a hug.

"Not bad," Mrs. Kim replied. "Except for Cleo asking 'When will we get there?' every two minutes."

As the grown-ups chatted, Maddie spotted Macy walking from the direction of Rosalyn's farm.

"You made it!" Maddie said.

"Thanks for inviting me," Macy replied. "Happy birthday, Evie." She held out a small gift wrapped in pretty paper.

Evie's eyes lit up. "Ooh! Thank you!" She took the present and started to pull off the bow.

"Hold on, Evie," Dad said. "Let's save the presents for when we have cake. Why don't you show Cleo around the farm, and then we'll have the tea party?"

Evie sighed. "Parents," she said with a shake of her head. "They always make you wait for presents."

Cleo nodded sympathetically.

As the two little girls ran off, Mom's cell phone pinged. Mom glanced at the message. "Oh no!" she said.

"What's wrong?" asked Maddie.

"Our special guest, 'Belle,' is having car trouble. She isn't going to make it to the party," Mom whispered.

"Can't we get someone else?" Maddie asked.

"Not this late." Mom sighed. "What a shame. At least Evie didn't know about it."

"What she doesn't know won't hurt her," Dad said. He turned to Cleo's parents. "Come on, let us show you around, too."

"Oh boy," Maddie murmured as the parents walked away.

"What's wrong?" asked Macy.

"Evie *did* know about Princess Belle coming. It was supposed to be a surprise, but she found out," Maddie explained. "She's going to be crushed."

"You have to tell her," Macy said.

"You think so?" Maddie asked.

Macy nodded. "Definitely. It would be worse if Evie thought Belle was coming but she never showed up."

"I guess you're right," Maddie said. "Come on, we'd better go find her."

They caught up with Evie and Cleo near the

pond. The little girls stood among the tall horsetail plants that gave Horsetail Hollow its name.

"This is our frog pond," Evie was saying. "Some of the frogs might be princes, but we don't know for sure. Mom says not to kiss them."

"Evie," Maddie interrupted.

Evie looked up. "Yeah?"

"I have some bad news," Maddie said gently.

"Princess Belle can't come. Her car—er, *carriage* broke down."

Evie blinked. "Oh."

Poor Evie, Maddie thought. Was she going to cry? To her surprise, Evie just nodded. "Okay."

"Really? You're not upset?" Maddie asked.

"Nah." Evie shrugged. She cupped her hands around Cleo's ear and whispered something. Cleo's eyes widened.

"Wow," Maddie said as the two little girls ran off, giggling. "That went way better than I expected."

Maddie suddenly felt better.

"Come on," she said to Macy. "I want to show you something."

A few minutes later, Maddie and Macy were sitting in the hayloft above the barn. They let their feet dangle out the open door as they looked out at the farm and the surrounding woods.

"You're right," Macy said. "The view is great from up here."

"Yeah." Maddie sighed happily.

"You're so lucky," Macy said. "You have a barn and a pasture. You have everything you need for a horse."

Maddie smiled. "Yeah. Except the horse. But I'm working on that," she added.

Macy sighed. "I wish I had a horse."

"What about Genie?" Maddie asked.

"I love Genie. But she's my grandma's horse. I want a horse that's mine." Macy leaned back on her hands. "If I had a horse, I'd ride her every single day. And I'd teach her to come when I called."

Maddie nodded. "Me too."

"I'd put braids in her mane," Macy went on. "And I'd name her Sunshine or maybe—"

"Lucky," the girls said in unison.

They looked at each other and smiled. Maddie had never had a friend her age who liked horses as much as she did. Suddenly she wanted to tell Macy all about Maximus and Angus.

But how could she? Macy would never believe it.

A sudden breeze stirred the trees. From overhead, they heard a loud creaking.

"What's that sound?" Macy asked.

Maddie looked up at the roof and gasped. "The weather vane!"

They could hear the rusty metal horse spinning round and round. There was only one thing that made the weather vane spin like that.

She stood up quickly. "Where are Evie and Cleo?"

"I saw them go that way a few minutes ago." Macy pointed in the direction of the wishing well.

"Oh no! We have to hurry!" Maddie ran for the ladder, with Macy on her heels.

But when they got to the well, no one was there.

The opening of the well was covered with a heavy cement lid. Maddie's parents had put it there to make the well safe. But there was still a gap big enough to slip a penny through.

Evie's favorite book of fairy tales lay open on top. Macy picked it up.

"Hey, 'Beauty and the Beast,'" she said. "I love this story."

Maddie's heart sank. Had Evie wished herself into the fairy tale—and taken Cleo with her?

"She wouldn't," Maddie whispered.

Oh yes, she would, her mind answered.

On the ground, something gleamed. Maddie looked closer. Three shiny pennies lay in the grass. Maddie realized they must have fallen from Evie's pocket.

Each wish needed a coin to make it come true. If Evie and Cleo were in the fairy tale without any pennies, how would they wish themselves back?

Macy was watching her with concern. "Is everything okay?" she asked.

"Evie and Cleo are lost. I need to find them," Maddie said.

"I'll help you," said Macy. "Where do you think they went?"

Maddie glanced at the picture in the storybook. "Not far, I hope."

She took a deep breath. She had just met Macy. Could she trust her with a secret as big as the wishing well?

Maddie picked up the pennies. She put two in her pocket. She held the third one out to Macy.

"We need to make a wish. Together," Maddie explained. "We need to wish ourselves to wherever they went."

Macy looked confused. "Um . . . shouldn't we just look in the barn or something?"

"Please," Maddie said. "Trust me."

Macy hesitated. Then she gave a little nod. She put her hand on Maddie's.

"On the count of three." Maddie closed her eyes. Macy did, too.

"One . . .

"Two . . .

"*Three.*"

CHAPTER
THREE

Maddie felt a warm breeze against her face. She
opened her eyes.

She and Macy were standing at the wishing well.
But Horsetail Hollow was gone.

The well now stood in the center of a small,
busy village. People hurried by on the narrow
cobblestone streets. Right away, Maddie could tell
they were from a different time and place. The men

wore ponytails and jackets with tails. The women wore dresses with aprons and funny little caps. They called out to one another as they passed.

"Bonjour!"

"Bonjour!"

A man bustled past, pushing a cart of freshly baked bread. "Marie! The baguettes! Hurry up!" he called into the window of a bakery.

Maddie stole a glance at Macy. She was gazing around, openmouthed with astonishment.

She's probably in shock, Maddie thought. *I'd better break it to her gently.* "Macy, that wish we just made? It brought us—"

"Into a fairy tale, I know!" Macy interrupted breathlessly. "It's exactly like I imagined."

"You imagined this?" It was Maddie's turn to be surprised.

"Of course! Didn't you ever read a good book and imagine you were in it?" Macy asked.

Maddie shook her head.

"Well, I do all the time. And fairy tales are my favorite." Macy put her hands on her hips. She looked around, suddenly businesslike. "So, where should we start?"

"Start what?" Maddie couldn't get over how well Macy was taking this.

"Looking for Evie and Cleo," Macy said.

"Oh! Right," Maddie said. "I guess we should just start asking people."

They wandered through the narrow streets. Women carrying baskets haggled with peddlers pushing wooden carts of fish and produce.

"I need six eggs!"

"That's too expensive!"

"You call this bacon?"

"What lovely grapes!"

A young girl went by herding a gaggle of geese. Maddie waved to her.

"Excuse me? Have you seen two little girls?"
she asked.

The girl gaped at them, then hurried away.

A cart horse went by, its hooves clopping loudly
on the cobbles. The driver gawked at Maddie and
Macy as he passed.

"Excuse me!" Maddie called to him.

But the driver just snapped the reins and sped on.

"The people here aren't very friendly, are they?"
Macy said.

"Maybe it's how we're dressed." Maddie looked
down at her jeans and T-shirt. "Too bad we didn't
wear princess gowns like Evie and Cleo—"

She snapped her fingers. "That's it!"

"What's it?" asked Macy.

"We're looking in the wrong place," Maddie
explained. "Evie and Cleo wouldn't be here in the
village. They'd be at the castle—with Princess Belle!
That's where we need to go! Come on, it must be
somewhere around here."

Maddie turned and almost bumped into someone coming from the other direction. It was a young woman wearing a simple blue dress and a white apron. She was reading a book as she walked. Maddie would have run right into her. But at the last second, the woman deftly stepped out of the way.

"Excuse me?" Maddie said.

The young woman looked up from her book. She had a pale, pretty face and brown hair that she'd tied back with a ribbon. She smiled when she saw Maddie and Macy.

"Bonjour," she said. "Can I help you?"

"Could you tell us the way to the castle?" Maddie asked.

"Um . . . Maddie?" Macy whispered.

The woman's brow furrowed. "The only castle around here is that way." She pointed to a rough dirt road that led into the woods. "But I can't imagine why you'd want to go there."

"We're looking for my sister and her friend," Maddie explained. "They're visiting the princess."

Macy tugged her sleeve. "Maddie . . ." she whispered a little louder.

The woman looked perplexed. "But the castle has been abandoned for years."

"Ohhhh," Maddie said as the truth dawned on her. The villagers didn't know about Belle and the Beast yet! "Right. Thank you, anyway."

"You're welcome." The woman put her nose back in her book and continued on her way.

"Well, she was nice," Maddie said, watching her go.

Macy looked at her in disbelief. "Maddie! *That* was Belle!"

"Her?" Maddie squinted at the young woman's back. "She doesn't look anything like a princess."

"That's because she's not a princess—yet," Macy said. "Don't you know this story?"

"Of course, I do! I mean, sort of . . . not really," Maddie admitted. "Fairy tales are more Evie's thing."

"It's a good thing I'm here. Before Belle meets the Beast, she's just a villager. She doesn't become a princess until *after* they fall in love," Macy told Maddie.

"Well, that explains her boring dress," Maddie said. "But if Belle's not at the castle, and Evie and Cleo aren't with Belle, that means . . ."

Maddie's eyes widened. Macy's did, too.

"They're at the Beast's castle—alone," Macy said.

CHAPTER
FOUR

"Are you sure this is the right way?" Macy asked.

Maddie paused. She looked around. "I think so."

They had been walking for some time. But they seemed to be going deeper and deeper into the woods. Maddie wished they had asked Belle for better directions.

Something rustled in the bushes nearby. Maddie jumped. She clutched Macy's arm. "What was that?"

The leaves rustled again. A small bird burst from the bush and flew away.

"Stop jumping," Macy told Maddie with a frown. "Your jumping is making me jumpy."

"I can't help it," Maddie said. The woods were dark and spooky. Maddie kept thinking she saw shadows moving among the trees. But when she looked, nothing was there.

Macy rubbed the goose bumps on her arms. "Do you think they're looking for us?" she asked.

"Who?" asked Maddie.

"Your parents and Gram," Macy said.

Maddie hadn't thought of that. If their parents were looking for them, they would be very worried by now. But maybe they weren't looking. "The last time Evie and I visited a fairy tale—"

"Wait." Macy stopped walking. "You've done this before?"

"Lots of times. Well, twice anyway," said Maddie.

"And you didn't get in trouble?" Macy asked.

Maddie shook her head. "When we got home it seemed like hardly any time had passed," she explained.

Macy thought about this. "Let's keep going. Maybe the castle's just ahead!"

Macy started to run. So did Maddie. They had not gone far when they came to a fork in the road.

In one direction, the road was wide and straight. The sky above seemed brighter. The other road curved, turning deeper into the dark forest.

"We should go that way," Maddie and Macy said, pointing in opposite directions.

Maddie peered at the road Macy had chosen. Tree branches curled over it like bent claws. A cold wind blew dead leaves across the path. "*That* way? Are you serious?"

Macy folded her arms. "Who knows the story, me or you?"

Maddie put her hands on her hips. "Well, we're looking for *my* sister."

"You're just scared," Macy said.

Maddie scowled. "I am n—" She broke off with a gasp. "What's that?"

A thundering sound was coming toward them.

Hoofbeats! Maddie thought.

Suddenly, a horse came tearing around the bend in the road. It was pulling a cart.

But something was wrong. The cart had no driver!

The cart held a large object under a tarp. Every time the cart went over a bump, the object rattled and banged. The noise made the terrified horse run faster.

Maddie and Macy jumped out of the way as the horse flew past. The cart swerved dangerously.

At that moment, one of the wheels hit a deep rut. The cart tipped. One of the cart shafts came loose and struck the horse's back legs.

The horse squealed with fear. He reared, trying to get free.

"We have to help him. He's going to get hurt!" Maddie said.

"How?" Macy asked. "If we get close, *we* might get hurt."

Maddie knew Macy was right. The horse was a huge Belgian draft. Maddie guessed he weighed two thousand pounds, maybe more. His hooves were as big around as her head.

They watched the horse struggle. His shrill, frightened whinnies were awful to hear.

"If I can get him to calm down, I might be able to unhitch the cart," Maddie said. "I have to try."

"Be careful," Macy said.

Maddie slowly approached the horse. "Easy, fella," she murmured. "Don't be afraid. I'm trying to help."

Was it her calm voice? Or was the horse just

exhausted? Whatever the reason, he stopped rearing. He watched Maddie with wary eyes.

"It's working. Keep talking!" Macy said.

"That's a good horse. Just hold still." Maddie took another step.

She had been studying the harness. A leather strap with a buckle held the cart shaft. Maddie inched forward. She reached out her hand.

"Got it!" Maddie released the buckle. The shaft fell free.

The horse sprang forward. He galloped away without a backward glance.

"So long, fella," Maddie said softly.

Macy came to stand next to her. "I can't believe you did that," she said. "I'm sorry for what I said before, about you being scared. You were really brave just now."

"You were right," Maddie admitted. "I *am* scared. I'm scared of these woods. I'm scared of that road.

I'm scared we won't ever find Evie and Cleo. But," she added, "I'm glad you're here with me."

"Friends?" Macy asked.

"Definitely," Maddie said.

Maddie linked her arm through Macy's. Side by side, they started down the road.

Even though the woods were dark, Maddie's heart felt light. She had a new friend!

CHAPTER
FIVE

As they went deeper into the woods, the air seemed to grow colder. The wind whistled in the trees. The puddles in the road had thin layers of ice.

The girls had only gone a short way when Maddie jumped again. "What was that?"

This time, Macy clutched her arm. "I heard it, too!"

They held still, listening.

Clip-clop.

Clip-clop.

Clip-clop.

The girls spun around. The big Belgian horse was following them!

"What's he doing here?" Macy wondered.

"I don't know. Maybe he's lost. Are you lost?" Maddie asked him.

The horse just looked at them. He had a white blaze on his forehead and large, gentle eyes. A thick blond forelock flopped over his brow.

"Let's try to get him to come to us," Macy said. She reached into her pocket and pulled out a peppermint candy.

"Do you always keep peppermints in your pocket?" Maddie asked.

"I do when I'm with horses." Macy unwrapped the candy. She held it out on her palm.

The horse's nostrils quivered. He took one step forward, then another.

Slowly, the horse came to Macy. He put his nose to her hand. His breath steamed out. Then he nibbled up the candy.

"I think we made a friend," Maddie said.

"Lucky for us he has a sweet tooth," Macy said.

The girls petted the horse's thick blond mane. Maddie noticed an engraved plate on his bridle.

"*Philippe*," she read. "Is that your name?"

The horse's head bobbed, as if to say, *That's right.*

"Well, I'm glad to meet you, Philippe. But I still don't know what you're doing here," Maddie said.

"Maybe he's here to help us. Just like 'The Lion and the Mouse'!"

Maddie turned with a gasp. "What lion?"

"Not here, silly. The story. You know, the lion lets the mouse go free. And then one day the mouse comes back to help the lion." Macy waved her hand impatiently. "The point is, we helped Philippe, and now he's come to return the favor!"

"Maybe," said Maddie. *Or maybe he just doesn't want to be alone,* she thought.

"Is that it?" she whispered to the horse, stroking his mane. "Are you afraid to be out here alone?"

The horse nickered softly.

"Do you think he'll let us ride him?" Macy asked.

"Let's try," Maddie said. "I'll help you up."

She cupped her hands to make a step, then boosted Macy onto Philippe's back.

Once she was in the saddle, Macy reached down and helped Maddie up.

As soon as they were both on his back, Philippe

57

turned and started walking in the direction of the village.

"Not that way, Philippe. This way!" Maddie said, turning him around.

But Philippe didn't want to go that way. He yanked at the reins, turning back toward the village.

Back and forth they went. Maddie pulled the reins one way. Philippe went the other.

"Philippe!" Maddie cried at last. "If you want to go that way, then go. But Macy and I are going to the Beast's castle. Like it or not."

Philippe lowered his head. He heaved a sigh, as if to say, *I don't like it at all. But I'll do it.*

"Is it just me, or is it getting colder?" Maddie asked. Her hands were so cold she could barely hold the reins.

"It's definitely colder. Look." Macy pointed. White flakes drifted down from the sky.

"Snow!" Maddie exclaimed. "But it was summer in the village!"

Philippe plodded along nervously. His head was high. His ears flicked left and right, alert to any danger.

"I'm freezing," Macy said. "Can't Philippe go any faster?"

"I'm trying." Maddie gave him another kick. But Philippe just continued to creep along, startling at every sound. She had never met such a skittish horse.

Suddenly, something burst from the underbrush. It darted across their path.

Philippe spooked.

"It's just a rabbit!" Maddie cried as the hare hopped away.

But it was too late. Philippe took off running.

"Whoa, Philippe! *Whoa! WHOA!*" Maddie cried, tugging at the reins.

The horse only went faster. They flew over a fallen tree and around a bend. Suddenly, Philippe skidded to a stop.

A tall iron gate blocked their path. If they'd stopped a second later, they would have crashed into it.

Maddie and Macy slid down from Philippe's back. All three stared through the bars of the gate.

"Whoa," Maddie said quietly.

Through the falling snow they could see an enormous palace. Tower after tower stretched toward the gray sky.

"The Beast's castle," Macy said.

CHAPTER

SIX

Maddie looked at Macy and Philippe. "Are you ready?"

"Ready," whispered Macy.

Philippe nickered, as if to say, *Must we do this?*

"I have to find my sister," Maddie said. She tried the iron gate. It opened with a creak. "Everybody stay close," she whispered.

She crept through the gate. Macy followed. Philippe brought up the rear.

They found themselves in an immense garden. Statues stood among the frozen hedges, the snow piling softly on their marble heads. Maddie saw a bed of roses frozen in midbloom. Their petals showed red beneath the frost.

As they crept through the garden, Maddie kept an eye out for the Beast. But all was quiet. The castle and grounds seemed silent as a tomb.

"Look," Macy said, pointing.

Two sets of small tracks made a path through the snow. They led right up to the castle entrance.

"Those must be Evie's and Cleo's footprints!" Maddie said.

Philippe snorted, as if to say, *They walked right up to the front door?*

Maddie was about to follow the tracks. But Macy stopped her. "Wait," she said. "The Beast could be waiting for us. Let's try to find another way in."

Maddie nodded. "Good thinking."

On the side of the castle, Maddie spotted a small wooden door half-hidden by vines. She put a finger to her lips and pointed.

The girls and Philippe sneaked toward the door. Philippe lifted his hooves high. He was trying to tiptoe!

When they got to the door, Macy tried the handle. It was unlocked. She pushed open the door and crept inside. Maddie followed. Philippe tried to follow, too.

"Horses aren't allowed inside. You have to stay here," Maddie told him.

Philippe gave her a panicked look. *You're leaving me alone?* his eyes seemed to say. He tried again to squeeze past Maddie.

But the doorway was narrow. And Philippe was a very big horse. He didn't make it far.

"Philippe, I promise we won't let anything happen to you," Maddie said, petting him. "Do you trust me?"

Philippe sighed. *I trust you,* he seemed to say. Then he stomped a hoof as if to add, *But please hurry!*

Maddie stepped inside and shut the door. As soon as it closed, they found themselves in the dark.

"I can't see anything!" Macy whispered.

Maddie found Macy's hand in the dark. "Come on. I see a light ahead."

The two girls made their way toward it. Three candles burning in a holder sat in an alcove.

Maddie picked up the candelabra and held it aloft. She could now see they were in a narrow corridor. "That's better."

"Bonjour," said a voice in her ear.

Maddie gasped and spun around. The hallway was empty.

To Maddie's horror, the candelabra in her hand suddenly squirmed. "Not so tightly, s'il vous plaît," it said.

Maddie dropped it with a shriek. The candles went out.

But a second later, the candelabra hopped to its feet. Its flames flickered back to life.

"Welcome," it said, gesturing with a candlestick. "We have been expecting you."

"It's haunted!" Maddie turned to run. But Macy grabbed her arm.

"Not haunted, Maddie. *Enchanted*," Macy said. "You really don't know your fairy tales, do you?" She turned to the candelabra. "I'm Macy, and this is Maddie. We're sorry to intrude. We're just looking for our friends."

"Enchantée." The candelabra bowed deeply. "I am Lumiere."

"No, no, no!" said another voice.

A squat little clock waddled into the light. Maddie stared. The clock's face had a *face*. Its hands looked like a drooping moustache.

"No more visitors!" the clock huffed.

"Please excuse Cogsworth," Lumiere said to Maddie and Macy. "He's very tightly wound today. Now, if you will follow me. Right this way."

Lumiere turned and started away, hopping down the hallway on his single foot. Maddie and Macy had no choice but to follow.

The passageway was narrow and damp. It smelled of mildew. Maddie passed through a cobweb and shivered.

Were they being taken to the dungeon? she wondered. Was that where they'd taken Evie and Cleo?

Poor Evie! Poor Cleo! They must be so scared!

The corridor grew warmer. Maddie smelled something delicious. Was it—chocolate cake? It couldn't be, Maddie thought. What sort of dungeon had chocolate cake?

A moment later, they stepped into a large, warm room. Heat radiated from a big cast-iron stove in the corner.

In the middle of the room, a table was set for tea. Maddie stopped. Her mouth fell open in surprise.

There sat Evie and Cleo. They were shoveling cake into their mouths as fast as they could. But they looked up when Maddie and Macy walked in.

Cleo waved a fork. "Hi, guys!"

"Guess what?" Evie said through a mouthful of whipped cream. "You're just in time for dessert!"

CHAPTER

SEVEN

"Dessert?" Maddie exclaimed. She felt heat rising in her face, and it wasn't only from the warm room. "Are you *kidding me*, Evie?"

"What?" Evie asked innocently.

"We have been looking all over for you!" Maddie cried. "And you're sitting here eating CAKE?"

"Well, it *is* her birthday," said a motherly voice. Maddie looked around to see who had spoken.

"Down here, dear." The teapot was talking.

A puff of steam curled from its spout. "I'm Mrs. Potts," the teapot said. "You mustn't be mad at Evie. The cake was my idea. When we heard it was her birthday, I thought we should celebrate. We've had so few happy birthdays here lately," she added a little sadly.

"We got to sing!" piped up a little chipped teacup. Like Mrs. Potts, the teacup had eyes and a mouth. The cup handle was where his nose would be.

The teacup burst into song. *"Happy birthday to you! Happy birthday to you! Happy birthday, dear Eeeeevieeee—"*

"That's enough, Chip, dear," Mrs. Potts said.

"*Happybirthdaytoyou*," Chip finished in a rush.

Suddenly, Maddie felt very tired. She plopped down in a chair. Macy sat down, too.

"Have some tea." Mrs. Potts poured them each a cup. Maddie wrapped her cold hands around the warm china. She took a small sip and felt better.

"I don't get it, Evie. Why are you here when there's a party waiting for you at home?" she said.

"We came to find Belle," Evie explained. "We were going to bring her to my party."

"But she isn't here. They don't even *know* her!" Cleo added in a loud whisper.

"Of course Belle's not here. We just met her in the village," Macy said.

Cogsworth, who had been pacing fretfully, now spoke up. "There you have it! She's in the village, not here! Better hurry and find this Belle person. Off you go!" He tried to shoo them toward the door.

"Don't rush our guests off, Cogsworth," Lumiere said. "You'll make them feel unwelcome."

"They are NOT welcome!" Cogsworth burst out. "If the Master finds out—"

"The Master?" Maddie said. "You mean the Beast doesn't know we're here?"

The servants exchanged uneasy glances.

"We thought it best not to tell him," Mrs. Potts said, lowering her voice. "I didn't want to frighten the little ones. But, you see, we had another visitor today. And the Master, he . . . well, he . . ."

"He threw him in the dungeon!" Cogsworth snapped. "And you'll all be next!"

Evie's blue eyes widened. "A man came here today?" she asked.

"Yes. All the poor man wanted was a rose for his daughter. I'm afraid the Master can be very cruel sometimes." Mrs. Potts looked pained.

Evie, Cleo, and Macy gasped in unison. "It's him!" Evie exclaimed.

"Am I missing something?" Maddie asked. "Who's 'him'?"

"Belle's father!" Evie explained. "Which means Belle will be here to rescue him any minute!"

"But we've been waiting and waiting. Why isn't she here?" Cleo asked.

"Well, it's a long walk from the village. We should know," Maddie said.

Evie rolled her eyes as if Maddie was hopeless. "Belle doesn't *walk*. She rides a horse! When her father gets captured, their horse runs home. That's how Belle knows something bad happened. The horse is the one who brings her here."

Maddie and Macy looked at each other. "Uh-oh," they both said.

"We met a horse on the way here," Maddie explained. "But it's probably a coincidence. Philippe doesn't seem like—"

"*Philippe?*"

Evie slapped her forehead. Cleo shook her head in disbelief.

"Philippe is Belle's horse," Cleo exclaimed. "*EVERYBODY* knows that!"

"We have to get him back to Belle right away! Where is he now?" Evie asked.

"He's right outside," Maddie said.

"By the servants' entrance?" Lumiere looked worried. "But that is right below the Master's terrace! The horse will be seen!"

"Hurry, girls! Hurry!" Mrs. Potts urged.

The four girls jumped up from the table. "Thank you," Evie said, kissing the teapot on the lid. The other girls quickly thanked her, too.

"It was my pleasure, dears," Mrs. Potts replied. "Come back and see us again. But now you must go!"

The girls said good-bye to Lumiere and Cogsworth. Then they ran back down the corridor to the exit.

Philippe was standing right where they'd left him. When the horse saw them, he whinnied with joy.

Maddie realized they had a new problem: They had four people and only one horse.

"Macy, you and Evie ride Philippe to Belle," she suggested. "Cleo and I can walk."

"But I want to meet Belle, too!" Cleo protested.

"Why don't Evie and Cleo take Philippe?" Macy suggested.

"We don't know how to ride!" exclaimed Evie.

Philippe stamped his hooves impatiently. *Will you please make up your minds?*

At that moment, a terrible roar split the air.

They all looked up. The Beast stood on a terrace above them. He was twice as big as a man, with a face like a lion. His body was covered with fur. Twisted horns grew from his head.

"Trespassers!" he roared, baring his fangs. "Come to stare at the Beast, did you?"

The sight was too much for Philippe. The horse gave a scream of fear and bolted.

"Philippe!" Maddie cried. "Wait for us!"

The girls ran, scrambling over the snowy ground. Maddie had almost reached the garden, when her foot slipped on a patch of ice.

"Ahh!" she cried as she sprawled in the snow.

She tried to stand and slipped again. Her heart pounded. The Beast was going to get her!

But when she looked back, the Beast was still

standing on the terrace. He looked down at Maddie.

But he no longer looked angry. His face was full of sadness.

Maddie felt a jolt of pity. Belle's father wasn't the only one trapped in the castle, she realized. The Beast was a prisoner there, too.

"Maddie, come on!" Macy had almost reached the gate.

With one last glance at the Beast, Maddie got to her feet and raced after Macy, Evie, and Cleo.

She caught up with them on the other side of the gate. Philippe and the other girls had stopped in the middle of the road. They were looking at something ahead.

"Thanks for waiting, guys!" Maddie said as she ran up. "I just realized something. The Beast isn't . . ."

The words died on her lips.

A huge gray wolf stood in their path. Now

Maddie knew why the others had stopped. The girls and Philippe were frozen with fear.

"Everyone stay calm. Let's all just back up slowly . . ." Maddie whispered.

Shadows moved among the trees. Three more wolves slipped out of the woods.

They were surrounded.

The wolves stared at them with hungry yellow eyes. Maddie huddled closer to Philippe. Not that the horse would be much help. He was trying to hide behind Evie.

"It's okay." Maddie tried to stay calm, but her voice shook. "Wolves aren't bad. That's just a myth. In real life, they hardly ever bother people."

"There's just one problem," Macy said. "This *isn't* real life!"

The wolves began to circle.

"Maddie?" Evie said. Her eyes looked big and scared. "What do we do?"

Maddie could think of only one thing.

"Help!" she screamed.

The other girls started yelling, too. "Help! Help! Help!"

But the castle was too far away. The falling snow muffled their cries. No help came.

The pack tightened their circle. *This is it,* Maddie thought. She felt dizzy with fear. The world seemed to spin.

But—*wait.* It wasn't just Maddie. The world *was* spinning!

The snowflakes swirled. The forest blurred. The circling wolves became streaks of gray. Maddie felt as if she was standing in the eye of a hurricane. All she could do was cling to Philippe.

When the spinning stopped, the forest, the

castle, and the wolves were gone. The girls were back in Horsetail Hollow. They were standing right next to the wishing well as if they'd never left. And Philippe was with them!

After the dark, snowy forest, the farm seemed strangely calm and bright. Maddie blinked in the sunlight. "But how did we—"

"Maddie! Evie!"

Maddie spun around. Dad was calling. He sounded annoyed.

"Dad!" Evie squealed, running toward him.

Dad turned. He hadn't seen them appear. "There you are! For Pete's sake, girls. I've been calling for ages. Didn't you hear me?"

"I . . . we . . ." Maddie stuttered.

Evie threw her arms around him. "It was so scary, Daddy! There were wolves!"

Dad raised his eyebrows. "Wolves?"

"We went to Belle's castle, and the Beast almost

got us!" Evie went on. "But the wolves were even scarier—"

Dad chuckled. "Another magical adventure, was it? But, Evie, it's time for your tea party. Though the tea's probably cold by now." He turned to Maddie and added, "I wish you'd come when I called. I was starting to get worried."

Wish? Maddie thought.

"Dad? Did you throw a penny in the well?" she asked.

"Oh. Yes, it was sitting on the edge. I knocked it in by accident. Sorry, kiddo. Here, take one of mine." He took a coin from his pocket and handed it to her.

Maddie stared at the penny in her palm. Had Dad just saved them . . . *by accident*?

"What is wrong with that horse?" Dad asked, suddenly noticing Philippe.

Philippe's knees were wobbling. His eyelashes

fluttered. All the excitement had been too much for the timid horse. He looked like he was going to faint.

Keep it together, Philippe! Maddie thought. She leaned against him to hold him upright. "Oh, he's fine."

"He doesn't look well," Dad remarked.

"He always looks like that," Macy added, propping Philippe up from the other side.

Behind Dad's back, Evie signaled urgently. *Belle!* she mouthed.

"But come to think of it, we should probably get him back, um . . . home," Macy added quickly.

"Back to your grandmother's house?" Dad asked. He'd mistaken Philippe for one of Rosalyn's horses. "That will take too long. Why don't you take him home after the party?"

The girls exchanged worried looks.

"Dad? Can we do the party another time?" Evie asked.

"Another time? Don't be silly! You've been waiting for this party for weeks. And Cleo came all the way from the city. Come on, girls. It's teatime!" Dad waved them on, and started back to the farmhouse.

The girls reluctantly followed, dragging the woozy horse with them.

At the house, Maddie left Philippe outside. "Wait here. We'll be right back." She put her face close to Philippe's and whispered. "Don't fall apart now, Philippe. You have a story to save!"

Inside, the girls took their places at the table. Mom raised her teacup. "Now that everyone's here, I'd like to make a toast to—"

"Done!" Evie slammed her empty cup down on the saucer. She'd swallowed her tea in one gulp.

The girls all hopped up from the table.

"Me too!"

"It was delicious!"

"I'm stuffed!"

"But you haven't eaten a bite!" Mom said.

"We're not hungry," Evie explained.

"Manners, girls," Dad reminded them. "We don't leave the table until everyone is finished."

As the parents nibbled their finger sandwiches, Maddie bounced her knees impatiently. She'd never seen anyone eat so slowly!

Macy fiddled nervously with her braids. Across the table, Cleo was wiggling in her seat. Evie looked ready to burst.

"What good sandwiches," Mr. Kim said.

"Have seconds," Mom said, passing the plate.

After what felt like an eternity, their parents pushed their chairs back from the table.

"Finally!" Evie cried. The girls jumped up and headed for the door.

"Not so fast," Mom said. "It's time for pictures!"

"*Pictures?*" the girls wailed in unison.

"We were better off with the wolves," Macy said under her breath.

"I have an idea! Let's take them with that darling horse!" Cleo's mom said, ushering everyone outside.

The parents lined the girls up in front of Philippe.

"Say cheese!" Dad exclaimed.

"Cheeeese," the girls said, grimacing.

A loud thump came from behind them. Maddie turned. Philippe had passed out cold!

"Oh, my goodness!" said Mrs. Kim.

"Oh no!" Evie whispered. "How is he going to help Belle now?"

"Wake up, Philippe," Maddie said gently. But the horse didn't move.

"We could throw a bucket of water on him," Dad suggested.

"Dad, no!" Maddie said. Philippe was such a scaredy-horse. He would never recover from the shock.

"I know!" Macy said suddenly. She reached into her pocket and pulled out a handful of candy. "Peppermints!"

"Will that work?" Maddie asked.

Macy shrugged. "It can't hurt."

Macy unwrapped the candies. She waved them under Philippe's nose. "Yum, yum, Philippe. Want a treat?"

Philippe's nostrils twitched. He opened one eye. Then he opened the other.

Philippe sat up. He ate all the candies out of Macy's hand.

Everyone cheered.

"Macy, you saved the day!" Maddie said, as Philippe slowly got to his feet.

Philippe nosed Macy as if to say, *Thank you.*

Macy took a little bow. "But I *really* think we should take Philippe home now," she said.

"That's a good idea." Dad nodded. "We'll wait to serve the cake until you're back."

The girls and Philippe ran back to the wishing well.

Maddie held up a penny. "We'll all wish together. On the count of three—"

"Wait!" Macy pointed to the book of fairy tales. On the page, wolves prowled through a dark forest. "How do we know we won't end up right back where we were?"

Philippe shuddered. He gave them a pleading look as if to say, *Don't send me back there.*

The girls looked at one another. "What do we do?" Evie asked.

"I have an idea," said Cleo.

She reached up and turned the page.

"Why didn't I think of that?" said Maddie.

She held out the penny. The other girls put their hands on Maddie's. Philippe added his hoof.

Then they closed their eyes . . . and *wished*.

CHAPTER
NINE

With a *whoosh*, the girls and Philippe found themselves back in Belle's village. They were standing in front of a simple stone house with chickens in the yard.

Philippe whinnied joyfully. *I'm home!*

The door of the house opened. Belle stepped out.

Evie and Cleo both gasped.

"It's really her," Cleo said, awestruck.

But Belle didn't notice them. She was looking

at Philippe. "What are you doing here, Philippe? Where's Papa?" she asked.

"We found Philippe in the woods!" Macy told her.

"Your father is being held prisoner in the castle!" Maddie exclaimed.

Belle's hand flew to her mouth in horror. "I have to go to him!"

"Philippe can take you. He knows the way. Hurry, there's no time to lose!" Maddie said.

Belle disappeared into the house. She returned a moment later wearing a long riding cloak. Quickly, she swung herself onto Philippe's back.

"She's *so cool*," Evie whispered.

"The best," Cleo agreed.

"Take me to Papa," Belle told Philippe.

But Philippe didn't move. His eyes looked frightened. *Not again!*

"Philippe, please hurry." Belle nudged him with her heels. "Why won't he go? What's wrong with him?"

Maddie could guess. Philippe knew what awaited them in the forest. He never wanted to go back.

"Try a peppermint," Macy said helpfully, holding one out to Belle.

But even the tasty treat wasn't enough to move Philippe. He hung his head and wouldn't budge.

"Can I try talking to him?" Maddie asked.

Belle nodded.

Maddie leaned close to Philippe. "You are a brave horse," she murmured.

Philippe hung his head and sighed. *No, I'm not.*

"You are," Maddie insisted. "You know how I know?"

Philippe kept his head down. But both his ears turned toward Maddie. She could tell he was listening.

"You weren't lost when we found you in the woods. I know that now," Maddie said. "You knew your way home. But you followed Macy and me to make sure we were safe."

Philippe looked up at her and nickered. *That was nothing.*

"I know how you feel," Maddie told him. "I'm scared lots of times."

She thought of the time she'd fallen off Angus. She'd been scared to ride after that. But she'd done it when Angus needed her.

She'd been scared to free Philippe from the cart, too. But she'd been *more* scared of what would happen if she didn't help him.

And going to the Beast's castle had been scariest of all. But she'd done it for Evie.

"Being brave doesn't mean you're not scared,"

Maddie said. She realized she was talking to herself as much as to Philippe. "I know you can do it, Philippe, and here's why: You have a big heart and you love Belle and her papa. *That's* what makes you brave."

Maddie leaned in close. She whispered right into Philippe's ear so only he could hear. "This story has a happy end, I promise. But *you* have to get it there."

Philippe closed his eyes and sighed. Had he given up? Maddie wondered. Was he even listening?

But then Philippe slowly raised his head. He had a determined look in his eye. He shook his mane and pawed the ground as if to say, *I'm ready.*

"Go, Phillipe!" Belle cried. They started to charge off. But suddenly Belle reined him in and looked back.

"How can I thank you?" Belle asked Maddie.

"It's nothing. I—" Maddie broke off as she caught sight of Evie and Cleo.

"Actually, there is *one* thing." She walked closer and whispered to Belle.

Belle looked surprised. "But I don't know any princesses," she said.

Maddie smiled. "Maybe someday you will. When you're ready, we'll be easy to find. Just go to the wishing well and make a wish." She pressed a penny into Belle's palm.

Belle put the coin in her cloak. Then she gave Philippe a kick. Together, they galloped away.

"Bye, Belle," Evie said softly.

Cleo sighed. "We never even got to talk to her."

"Who knows? Maybe you'll meet again someday," Maddie said.

"But it won't be my birthday," Evie said sadly.

Maddie put her arm around Evie. "I think we can still find a way to make the day special. Come on, guys. Who's hungry for birthday cake?"

CHAPTER
TEN

Back in Horsetail Hollow, Maddie, Evie, Macy, and Cleo walked slowly back to the farmhouse.

Maddie thought she had never been so tired. That day they had walked for miles, met a Beast, escaped a pack of wolves, and helped a nervous horse find his courage—and it was only half past noon.

"I need a nap," Cleo said.

"Me too," said Evie. "Can we skip the rest of my party?"

"No way," Maddie said. "We haven't even sung 'Happy Birthday' yet."

"Mrs. Potts and Chip and Lumiere sang it at the castle," Cleo reminded them.

"Just try to stay awake through the cake," Maddie said. "Then you can sleep as long as you like."

"There they are!" Dad said as the girls straggled up. The grown-ups were sitting at the large picnic table outside. The chocolate cake sat in the center of the table. It had seven candles waiting to be lit.

"Did you get Philippe home?" Mom asked.

"What? Oh. Yes." Evie yawned loudly.

The girls sat down at the table. Dad lit the candles. And everyone started to sing.

"Happy birthday to you . . .

"Happy birthday to you . . ."

Evie barely seemed to hear. She stared at the flickering candles with sleepy eyes.

"Happy birthday, dear Evie . . .

"Happy birthday to youuuu."

On the last note, Evie blew out the candles. Everyone clapped. Then, Maddie noticed another sound.

Clip-clop.

Clip-clop.

Clip-clop.

Evie heard it, too. She looked up from the cake. Her mouth fell open in surprise.

A beautiful princess was riding toward them on a handsome chestnut horse. The princess wore a long yellow gown. Her brown hair was piled in coils on her head. The horse wore a splendid saddle and a bridle with gold ornaments.

"Belle! Philippe!" Evie cried.

The girls all leaped up from the table. When he saw them, Philippe whinnied joyfully.

"I'm sorry I'm late," Belle said as she dismounted. She held out a red rose. "Happy birthday, Evie."

Evie put the rose to her nose and sniffed. Maddie had never seen her look so happy.

Belle turned to Mom, Dad, and Cleo's parents. "I don't believe we've met. I'm Belle," she said.

"Of course you are," Mom said with a big smile. "We didn't think you were coming."

"But we're so glad you made it," Dad added.

Belle nodded, then turned back to the girls. "Evie, I just love your dress."

Evie beamed. She grabbed Belle's hand. "Come meet the other Belle. She's a chicken!"

As Evie and Cleo pulled Belle away, Mrs. Kim leaned over to Mom. "That dress is amazing. She looks like a real princess!" she said.

"And the horse is a nice touch," Mom added.

Maddie looked at Macy. "Should we tell them?"

Macy shook her head. "Nah. Who would believe it?"

They went over to Philippe. Macy held out a peppermint. "How about a candy for old time's sake?"

Philippe ate it. Then he nuzzled them both. They wrapped their arms around his neck. Beneath the fancy bridle, he was the same sweet Philippe.

But Maddie noticed new confidence in his shining brown eyes.

"You did it, Philippe. I knew you could," Maddie told him.

Philippe nickered, as if to say, *Thanks to you.*

You helped me, too, Maddie thought. If not for Philippe, Maddie might never have known how brave she could be.

"You know, when you invited me to Evie's party, I had no idea it would be *this* exciting," Macy told Maddie.

"Me neither," Maddie said. "Are you still glad you came?"

Macy grinned. "I wouldn't have missed it for anything."

"Come on, everybody. It's time to eat cake!" Evie yelled.

They all gathered around the table—even Philippe. Belle sat between Evie and Cleo. Mom passed around slices of cake. She saved the biggest piece for Evie.

Evie took a big, chocolaty bite. "Best. Birthday. Ever!" she exclaimed.

Maddie looked around at all the new friends she'd made and smiled.

She had to agree.

Gallop away on the adventure of a lifetime with the Horsetail Hollow series: